Introduction

This book is not about good and evil.

It is about **control**, **inheritance**, and what happens when power outlives the structures that once contained it.

Wend is not magic.
It is not skill.
It is not belief.

It is a condition, rare, inherited, and neutral.
A space between breaths where action precedes intention.
This story follows three generations shaped by that space.
Astraea and Caelum learned to survive it.

Their children were shaped by it.
And an organization called Darth tried and failed to own it.

What follows is not a hero's journey.
There is no redemption arc.
There is only consequence.

This is the first movement in a three-part cycle.
The beginning of separation.
The recognition of inheritance.

And the slow, unavoidable correction that follows.
Read accordingly.

WEND

WEND

GARY HAYWOOD

GH WOOD LLC

1   BLACKOUT

The figure in the alley never looked up.

The power box fed the building beside it, a warehouse converted quietly, without permits, without questions. He opened the panel, studied the wiring for less than a second, and seated a device deep inside the housing.

Five minutes.

The panel closed.
The alley returned to stillness.

Inside the warehouse, production continued.
Long tables. Stainless trays. Industrial lighting that flattened color and erased individuality. Powder measured, funneled, sealed into vials. The women worked silently, masks, gloves, aprons. Clothing was minimized to reduce contamination. Routine had replaced modesty long ago.
Three men oversaw the floor.
Two discussed logistics, shipments, margins, deadlines that mattered only to those above them. The third leaned too close to one of the women, smiling, speaking softly as if familiarity could be negotiated.
She did not respond.
She kept working.
The lights went out.

Not an explosion.
Not a surge.
Absence.
No one screamed.
They were trained for outages. Product was covered. Timers checked. One man muttered and reached for his flashlight.
The one flirting never finished his sentence.

Something passed through him, so fast it displaced the air without sound. Not a strike. Not a grab.

A passage.

He folded inward and collapsed before his body understood it was done.
The woman behind him felt it.
Not hands.
Not breath.

A **wend**.

Nothing else.
Minutes fractured.
A low groan echoed once, then stopped.
The remaining two men drew their weapons. One moved toward the rear, toward the electrical room. The other swept the floor with a narrow beam, calling a name he already knew would not answer.
The light found a body.
Wrong posture.
Too much blood.
No struggle.
His breath caught.
Then his partner's light snapped off.

A dull sound followed, brief, wet.

Silence returned.

He stood alone.

Not afraid.

Calculation failed first.

Two equals gone. Less than a minute. No footsteps. No sound. No warning.

Air shifted.

A **wend** brushed past his ear.

He turned.

Everything went dark.

20 Years Earlier

The compound had no name.

Maps showed a blank where it should have been, mountain shadow, terrain labeled *inaccessible* by people who had never tried hard enough. The country around it changed flags every few decades. Discipline inside did not.

The boy was ten.

Too young to understand why he had been selected. Old enough to understand refusal was irrelevant.

Training began before explanation.

Before purpose.

Every morning started the same way. Bare feet on cold stone. Spine aligned. Eyes forward. Breath counted not in numbers, but in absence.

Breathe in.

Hold.

The instructors used a word sparingly. Never defined. Never emphasized.

A void.

The boy did not understand it. At ten, void still meant *nothing*. He had not yet learned that nothing could be shaped.

Breathe out.

Movement followed breath, but never during it. That was the rule. Action inside breath was crude. Wasteful. What mattered happened **between**.

He failed constantly.

Too early. Too late. Too visible.

Correction followed immediately. Silent. Exact. Not punishment, alignment.

Focus was trained before strength.

They ran him until his legs shook, then demanded stillness. They struck slowly, then required response faster than fear. They deprived him of sleep, then made him sit unmoving for hours, counting breaths that refused obedience.

Even when training ended, it did not end.

Walking was measured. Eating was measured. Watching others was measured. He was taught to observe motion, not people. Weight shifts. Micro-pauses. The space before decision.

At night, he sat alone.

Breathe in.

The void did not come.

Memory did.

Homes he barely remembered. A sister whose absence felt structural. The instructors said nothing. This part could not be taught.

Wend required something they could not install.

Focus so complete it erased self.

Will strong enough to act without desire.

Character stable enough to remain neutral.

Because wend was not a weapon.

It was a condition.

Between breaths, force could pass without announcing itself. Between breaths, motion could occur without effort. Between breaths, intent could exist without emotion.

The space did not care *why* it was used.

Good.

Evil.

Correction.

Erasure.

Labels failed here.

The boy learned slowly.

Some students wanted power. They failed.

Some wanted survival. They failed.

Some wanted approval. They failed.

He wanted nothing.

That unsettled the instructors.

At ten, he could not sustain the space. He could only touch it, briefly, accidentally. A step landing where it shouldn't. A strike passing too close without sound.

They did not praise him.

They increased difficulty.

Years later, they would argue whether he had been shaped, or whether he had simply endured long enough to reveal what was already there.

That night, lungs burning from controlled stillness, he understood only one thing:

Breathe in.

Hold.

There was something **between**.

And one day, he would learn how to move there.

3

Before the Void had a Name

They were never meant to meet.

Their clans had erased each other through attrition, records burned, bloodlines severed, victories claimed by silence. Encounters ended with bodies and no witnesses.

When Darth intervened, balance ended.
It did not recruit them.
It **claimed** them.

Taken separately. Folded into operations so deniable even their clans denied knowledge of them. Darth cared only about outcome.
They were top-tier wend users before the term existed in doctrine. Not because they were taught better, but because they survived long enough to refine what others approximated.

Wend had no master.
That was the lie people told themselves.
In truth, wend revealed preference.
The man's form was ruthless economy. Straight lines through space. Compressed. Final. He shortened rooms. Reduced options.
The woman's curved.
Timing bent around her. Distance misaligned. Opponents died believing they had misjudged proximity, not that she had ever been there.
Neither violated rules.

They interpreted them.

When Darth discovered their origins, rival clans, it engineered collision.

The assignment was framed as containment.

Neutralize a destabilized asset.

No extraction.

They recognized each other instantly.

Not faces.

Patterns.

Hatred had been inherited before language.

Their fight lasted less than a minute.

Wend folded against wend. Forms intersected without dominance. Each reached the same conclusion at the same moment:

Killing the other would cost too much.

Not emotionally.

Operationally.

They disengaged.

Darth observed.

Darth adjusted.

Joint operations followed. Controlled proximity. Rivalry sharpened restraint.

Their relationship did not soften.

It recalibrated.

Weeks became years. Their wend harmonized, not merged. Targets vanished. Systems collapsed quietly.

Then the twins were born.

Two heartbeats.

One rhythm.

The bloodlust ended, not through regret, but recognition.

Children introduced variables Darth could not model.

Their commitment to Darth did not break.

It **concluded**.

They vanished with permission no one else had ever received.

What remained were anomalies, timing gaps, surveillance failures blamed on equipment.

And two children born into silence heavy with inherited precision.

They never trained them.

Wend demanded choice.

And one day, one of those children would choose correction.

4
Divisions of the Same Silence

Astraea

Her name was rare.

Not for beauty.

For distance.

Training was filtration. Everything unnecessary was stripped away.

Pain clarified. Fear registered, then vanished. Compassion never arrived strongly enough to interfere.

She did not bond.

Attachment implied loss. Loss implied hesitation.

Her wend expressed early, vertical, decisive. Space obeyed without resistance.

The final trial was unannounced.

Four entered. One would leave.

The first attacked from fear.

The second from loyalty.

The third from desperation.

Astraea killed them in that order.

No waste. No flourish.

She stood where she had begun.

Complete.

5
Convergence

Caelum

His name carried weight.

His training demanded contradiction.

He was forced to break bodies while punished for desiring it. Forced to kill while evaluated for restraint.

He did not enjoy killing.

That was his flaw.

He imagined fatherhood structurally, teaching, protecting, building something that did not require erasure.

He buried that instinct.

Deep enough to fuel discipline.

His wend anchored space. When he moved, chaos paused long enough to end.

He killed without hatred. Without pleasure.

As breathing.

Afterward, he felt absence.

Space.

Years later, he would recognize it as the same place wend truly lived.

They were not paired by design.

That was the mistake.

They arrived at the same dead city chasing the same anomaly, an asset that had learned too much.

They sensed each other first.

Pressure.

Compression.

A mirrored threat.

They did not speak.

They moved.

Their first shared kill was accidental, two signatures converging so perfectly the body ceased before ownership mattered.

They paused.

Assessment.

They separated and continued as if the other were an environmental constant.

Death hesitated.

Darth reviewed the footage repeatedly.

They were paired again.

And again.

Not a team.

Parallel apex predators waiting for mirrored threats.

Entire networks folded in months.

Then trust emerged.

Unspoken.

Assumed.

Astraea left gaps Caelum occupied. Caelum delayed endings Astraea completed.

Attraction followed trust like an error in the math.

Proximity lingered.

Breath synchronized.

The most dangerous thing Darth had created was no longer singular.

It was relational.

And Darth had no protocol for that.

6   LEGACY PROTOCOL

D arth did not call it a final mission.

Endings were inefficient. Darth preferred *stabilization's,* actions framed as continuity rather than conclusion. But the internal brief carried markers Astraea and Caelum had never seen aligned.

Political trajectories.

Multi-decade projections.

Non-recoverable exposure thresholds.

This was not removal.

It was inheritance.

Every wend asset was deployed across the globe, quiet purges, sealed corridors, erased witnesses. Every operator except one. The omission was deliberate. A contingency held in reserve.

Astraea and Caelum were sent alone.

The island did not exist on civilian charts.

From above, it appeared inert. From below, engineered, layered defenses, automated turrets slaved to human oversight, machines that did not sleep and men trained not to hesitate.

They landed before dawn.

The first perimeter failed without registering breach. Sensors continued reporting normal conditions while guards stopped breathing where they stood.

Machines reacted faster.

Targeting re-calibrated. Fire corridors activated. Predictive models attempted to map movement.

They failed.

Wend did not exist inside the models.

Astraea collapsed distance so abruptly tracking systems followed empty space. Caelum anchored the environment just long enough for causality to resume, and end resistance.

Human guards fared worse.

Adaptation accelerated extinction.

Within minutes, the surface was silent.

They descended.

The compound's heart was buried beneath volcanic stone, carved where heat and pressure behaved incorrectly. The volcano below was not active, just restless enough.

The chemical was not synthesized.

It was harvested.

Naturally occurring only here, formed under pressure no laboratory could replicate. When refined, it produced results reports could not describe cleanly.

Subjects did not die.

They emptied.

Neural activity flattened without trauma. Consciousness evacuated without resistance.

Researchers stopped using the word *void*.

Not because it was inaccurate.

Because it was insufficient.

Astraea felt it immediately.

The air behaved like the moment before wend answered, except deeper.

Heavier.

Caelum slowed.

This place did not respond to wend.

It preceded it.

Darth wanted permanence.

A legacy enforced not by violence, but by erasure without death.

They completed the mission.

Data secured. Production sealed. Oversight transferred to structures meant to outlive governments.

Then they saw the exit protocols misaligned.

They were liabilities now.

Witnesses to the source.

Weapons too aware.

They exchanged no words.

Between breaths, trust held.

Elsewhere, untouched, the one wend user Darth had withheld felt recognition, not a summons.

Attention.

7 BETWEEN DETONATION AND SILENCE

The hours before departure were not marked by preparation.

They were marked by stillness.

The room was chosen for texture, not luxury. A four-poster bed anchored the space. Red satin caught low light like a held breath.

They did not ravage.
They experienced.

Each time felt like the first, not because memory failed, but because familiarity did not dull it. Love arrived not as escalation, but depth.

Their bond existed between detonation and sound, energy released before the world acknowledged it.

They looked into each other's eyes and did not look away.
Tears came without warning.

Recognition.
Passion layered without urgency. Wend had always demanded neutrality. This was something else entirely.
Impossible.

They separated only to move.
Naked. Facing one another.

Sparring, not as combat, but conversation. Balance answered balance. Timing met timing. Bliss braided with essence.

They laughed once.

Later, Astraea rested a hand where new life had begun.
Pregnancy did not weaken resolve.
It sharpened it.

This would be their last mission for Darth.
Disappearance was not escape.

It was completion.

Between breaths, they had found something wend could not erase.
And the void had competition.

8   THE SEVENTEEN HOUR PROTOCOL

D arth did not deploy soldiers.

It deployed conditions.
The compound had never been about ownership. It was a crucible.
The chemical had no official name.
Names suggested permanence.
Its lifespan inside the body was fixed, twenty-four hours. After that, degradation accelerated until collapse into gelatinous failure.

Death was not the objective.
Output was.

The first phase lasted three to six hours.
Trauma calibrated. Lightning-induced shock. Blunt force. Sensory overload. Rage cultivated.
Anger increased efficacy by one-point-five times.
Subjects who broke early were discarded.

Then came the *regulator*.
A woman. Calm voice. Gentle hands.
Her task was not mercy.
It was misdirection.
The subject always killed her.

Every time.

Afterward, the plateau began.

For seventeen hours, the subject entered a state no human baseline could match. No sleep. No hunger. No hesitation.

Unstoppable.

Collapse afterward was guaranteed.

The *Seventeen-Hour Protocol* was known to only two people.

This was why the island mattered.

Not nobility.

Continuity.

Power that obliterated everything it touched, for exactly seventeen hours.

Astraea and Caelum understood immediately.

This was succession.

And somewhere beyond containment, the protocol waited for something that would not break.

9   SEVENTEEN HOURS, MINUS ONE

They met it beneath the mountain.

Seven feet tall. No excess. No softness. Muscle wrapped bone with brutal efficiency. Eyes open and empty.

It screamed.

Not sound.

Pressure.

Wend collapsed.

Nullified.

They did not engage.

They ran.

Tunnels twisted downward. Smoke rolled thick. Fumes burned lungs and shortened time.

Behind them, it followed.

Relentless.

They seeded destruction as they moved, overloaded seals, collapsed storage, failed containment.

Then the mountain shifted.

A fissure cracked open below. Lava surged upward. Heat spiked.

The chemical turned volatile.

One spark from annihilation.
They turned.
They lured it downward, toward convergence.
They engaged.

Without wend.

Blows landed and meant nothing. Astraea struck stone. Caelum's ribs cracked.
They were losing.

Then Caelum stepped into Astraea's space.
Not beside.
With.
Breath matched. Weight aligned.
No doctrine.
Trust made kinetic.

They drove it backward into heat and vapor.
At the last moment, it tore free, vanishing into a flooded tunnel.
Then everything detonated.

Not fire.
Absence.

Caelum was thrown hard, consciousness shredding. Astraea felt heat bite her ankle, a touch that burned with unnatural glow.

No time.

She dragged him. Forced breath. Reached water.
They swam.
Behind them, the island folded into the sea.

The Seventeen-Hour Protocol ended.
Darth raged.
Astraea and Caelum vanished.
And somewhere in the deep, something else survived.

Waiting.

10 WHAT MOVES ABOVE THE WEND

The monks did not call it exile.

They called it preservation.

The boy was brought to the mountain compound before he was old enough to understand loss. By the time questions formed, answers were already unsafe. Names were withheld. Faces erased. Memory curated.

Not from cruelty.

From necessity.

The monastery existed beyond jurisdiction, older than borders, older than companies. It answered to no flag and no doctrine. Here, wend was not owned, branded, or weaponized. It was observed the way rare celestial events were observed.

With distance.

Once every one hundred and fifty years, deviation appeared.

Not mastery.

Precedence.

Someone whose relationship to wend was not movement *within* breath, but influence **above** it.

Most failed.

Some died.

A few lived, hollowed by contact they could not reconcile.

The boy trained daily.

At dawn, he sat on stone cold enough to enforce awareness. Breath slowed until it barely felt like his. Meditation here was not peace. It was endurance.

Breathe in.

Hold.

He felt something, but it was not the void the instructors described. It was quieter. Higher. As if the air itself waited.

He did not yet know wend.

His movements lagged behind command. Focus wandered. The instructors corrected carefully, never too much, never too fast.

They were afraid to rush him.

Because when he failed, the air reacted.

Not violently.

Respectfully.

They named him **Aurelion:** *Above the wend. Beyond the current.*

He did not understand the weight of it.

Only that when he stood still long enough, the world listened.

At night, elders reviewed fragments of forbidden history, twin births, mirrored signatures, pairings that destabilized eras.

They knew what had happened before.

And what had not yet arrived.

Somewhere else, unseen, another child existed.

A twin.

Her name would mean the opposite.

Together, they would not replicate their parents.

They would exceed them.

The monks said nothing.

Training continued.

Above the mountain, the air shifted, slightly, as if acknowledging something older than doctrine had begun again.

The Years Between Vanishing

T hey left with intention.

After the sea closed behind them, Astraea and Caelum swam until burning lungs became irrelevant. The boat waited where it had been anchored, far enough from probability to survive coincidence.

They sailed without chart.

The island they chose did not require a name.

There, time softened.

The twins were born beneath open sky. A boy and a girl. Healthy. Silent. Watching. Astraea held them first and felt it immediately, two complete signatures already aligned.

For a time, they were simply parents.

Life measured itself in mornings. Laughter replaced silence. Training disguised itself as play.

Too early, things happened.

At two, balance preceded falling.

At three, storms calmed accidentally.

Not wend.

Something prior.

Together, the twins did impossible things without knowing they had done anything at all. When one cried, air quieted. When one stumbled, ground rose.

Their connection was structural.

Astraea watched.

Caelum pretended not to.

Both understood.

Years passed anyway.
At nine, the world intruded.
A village. Too close. A mistake.
The girl wandered ahead. The boy lingered behind.

Her name was **Chora**.

That which lies beneath.
Foundation.
Where force gathers.
The bully was older. Bigger. Confident in borrowed cruelty. He
shoved Chora. She fell. He laughed. Then kicked her.
Her brother felt it instantly.
Distance did not matter.
He arrived calmly. She was bruised, breathing unevenly.

Chora smiled.
They were close enough now.
Thought aligned. Breath matched.
He knelt.
Together, they inhaled.
Bruises faded. Bone remembered itself.

Light flashed.
The bully struck stone and forgot how to breathe.
Astraea felt it from the island.
Caelum felt it too.
They arrived moments later.
Astraea healed the boy completely. Memory dulled.
The villagers spoke.

Leave.
Do not return.

That night, Astraea and Caelum did not sleep.
The *Seventh Sun* was discussed quietly.
But Chora was different.
Sharper. Faster. Always half a step ahead, and incomplete alone.

Separation would break them.
Keeping them together would break the world.

For the first time, they were disheartened.
Not afraid.
Grieving.
They loved their children enough to choose distance.

And hoped, one day, the twins would understand.

1 2

Graves That Do Not Answer

T he cemetery was quiet.

Cora stood between two markers.

Astraea.　　　　　Caelum.

She was somewhere in her twenties now. Old enough that grief should have dulled. Young enough that it hadn't.
The last time she saw them, she was eighteen.
Prepared. Armed. Finished.
She had not forgiven them.

Not for sending her brother away.

Not for silence.
She left anyway.
Five years later, Darth found them.
Details were fragments. Missing time. Only certainty remained.

Her brother had been gone longer.
She knew he lived.
That thin connection persisted.
Knowing was not finding.
She knelt, forehead against stone.
She remembered the word she first overheard.
Darth.

Later, by accident, she found records.
Too late.
Tears fell unchecked.
Then stillness returned.

"I'll find him," she said quietly. "Cost doesn't matter."

Her eyes hardened.
Far away, her brother felt something shift.
Not warning.
Alignment.
Cora turned away.
Stillness wrapped around her.
Together, they would finish what their parents delayed.

13

What Was Left at the Gate

A urelion was ten when they left him.

Old enough to feel abandonment.

Young enough to mistake it for betrayal.

The monastery gates closed without ceremony.

He was angry.
At his parents.
At silence.
His sister was alignment itself.
And now she was gone.
What prevented hatred was one moment.
His father knelt.

"You won't understand this now," he said. "Together, you're too much for the world. You need time apart to become balanced."
Hands cupped his face.
"We love you. Be strong. You will see your sister again. Take heart."

His mother echoed it.
They did not look back.
Years passed.
Training shaped discipline from rage. Stillness hurt more than combat.

Then certainty arrived.

His parents were dead.

He wept uncontrollably.

He knew two things.

They were gone.

His sister lived.

Training ended.

When he chose to leave, no one stopped him.

One monk asked him to stay.

Alaric.

"I knew your parents," he said.

Not as civilians.

As weapons.

Darth. Operations without names. Astraea and Caelum as instruments.

"I was their handler," Alaric said. "Their witness."

Then the truth.

There were no other wend users left.

Darth had broken them.

Astraea and Caelum killed the last.

Darth killed them for it.

"And your sister," Alaric said, "is the last known wend user alive."

The power between you is exponential.

Meet unbalanced, and you destroy everything.

Aurelion stood.

"I will find my sister. I will stay balanced. And I will end Darth."

He left.

The memory at the gate returned.

This time, it guided him.

Above the mountain, the air shifted, not in response, but recognition.

14
BLACK BOX

They did not have names.
Names created records.
Records created exposure.
Within Darth, they were designated only as:

Operative One and **Operative Two**.

Male.
Female.

Both nothing special.
Both unseen.
They answered to no hierarchy because Darth had none. There was no executive chain to sever, no board to indict. Darth functioned as a distributed organism, cells acting independently, coordinated by outcome rather than authority.
Operative One and Operative Two were its black box.
They controlled their own budgets.
Their own security.
Their own erasures.
Once, Darth had been built around wend users.
That era was over.
The research remained.
They had mapped everything, neurological quiet, movement between breaths, the strange inheritance that allowed certain bodies

to step where causality loosened. They traced origins. Correlations. Bloodlines.

And failed.

Every attempt to train ordinary humans collapsed. Discipline did not matter. Intelligence did not matter. Faith did not matter. Wend could not be learned.

It was inherited.

That bloodline, as far as Darth knew, was extinct.

Astraea and Caelum had been the last.

Their deaths had ended it.

Or so Darth believed.

What remained were experiments.

Failures stacked into budgets.

The closest approximation came from prisons and black sites. Psychopaths proved most compatible, not for strength, but chemistry. Rage remained unfiltered. Empathy did not interfere.

They injected the synthetic compound.

Normal humans died instantly.

Psychopaths transformed.

Briefly.

Muscle hardened beyond biology. Strength spiked into absurdity. Intelligence collapsed. What remained was motion and violence.

Ten minutes.

Sometimes twenty.

Never thirty.

No control. No direction.

Bones shattered under their own force. Teeth became weapons. When the compound burned out, the subjects collapsed into ruined flesh.

Dead.

It wasn't a protocol.

Protocols implied control.

This was chaos.

Budgets did not survive chaos.

Operative One watched another subject destroy itself on loop.

"We're out of time," he said.

Operative Two didn't look away. "We're out of excuses."

Then the message arrived.

Ten years late.

Perfectly timed.

A monk.

A quiet investment, one million routed through deniable channels. He had promised information *one day*.

That day had arrived.

Operative Two read the transmission twice.

Then again.

"He's the son," she said.

Operative One leaned forward.

"Of Astraea and Caelum. Their handler oversaw his training."

Silence.

The bloodline hadn't ended.

It had hidden.

Six million more cleared immediately.

"If he leaves the monastery," Operative One said, "we may never find him."

Operative Two smiled. "Then we intercept him."

Darth had just remembered how to hunt.

15
Descent

W ater filled Chora's mouth.

Salt. Cold. Weight.

She broke the surface once, just long enough to pull in air that burned, then slipped under again. Panic flared, sharp and immediate, then collapsed into discipline.

Control.

Everything is proceeding according to plan, she thought.
Then questioned it.
Whose plan?
The sea rolled above her like a ceiling that refused stability. She slowed her breathing until it felt imaginary.
Drowning was not an option.

"Aurelion would be pissed," she thought, smiling despite herself.

She reached into the dark.
Her gear should have been gone.
It wasn't.
Her fingers closed around it precisely, as if it had been waiting.
"Thank you," she murmured, to two ghosts who had taught her how to exist where others failed.

The suit sealed around her in practiced motions. Matte. Responsive. Alive to intent rather than pressure. This technology would have been useless to anyone else.

It required wend.

She had built it herself.

That still surprised her.

She was not an artist. Yet the schematics had flowed effortlessly, curves where rigidity failed, angles that made sense only between breaths.

Another quiet nod to her parents.

She descended.

Fast.

Gravity aligned instead of resisted. Darkness thickened. Pressure climbed.

Twenty minutes later, the seafloor revealed its scar.

Stone that did not belong.

Metal smothered in coral.

The facility.

Darth's facility.

The place where her parents' final mission had ended.

Chora hovered, suspended.

The water felt wrong, currents hesitant, sound distorted. As if the ocean remembered.

She angled downward.

The past waited below.

Chora was done waiting.

16
Ash and Afterimage

The monastery burned quietly at first.
Stone fractured.
Wood hissed.
Smoke folded inward, disciplined, as if even fire respected what it consumed.

Aurelion was already moving.

He felt it before impact, the pressure shift, the wrongness that preceded intrusion.

Elsewhere, Operative One watched the timer.

"Minus thirty minutes," he said, amused.

Operative Two smiled. "Plenty of time."

Three subjects breached the perimeter.

Victims.

Their bodies ran ahead of their minds. Muscle swollen. Jaws slack. Eyes empty.

The monks intercepted.

Calm.
Precise.

Unprepared.

Traditional wend failed, not fully, but enough. These things did not hesitate. They did not fear timing.

Necks snapped. Knees reversed. Spines folded.

Three was enough.

The compound fell.

Fire climbed the walls. Ancient halls collapsed into memory. Every monk died deliberately, each death purchasing seconds.
Time for one shadow to move unseen.

Aurelion reached the outer wall as the first structure failed.
He did not look back.
He jumped.
Air caught him, not as wend.
Something else answered.
Light erupted.
Not heat.
Not flame.
A white absence erased edges and burned shadow from existence. The creatures below vanished, removed before gravity could finish forming.
Two survived the night.
A broken monk.
And Aurelion, already gone.

Darth's recordings returned nothing.
Audio flattened.
Video smeared.
Telemetry contradicted itself.
Fragments remained.
A black figure.
A shadow moving through light.
Operative One struck the console.
"That power"
"If we could harness it," Operative Two finished.
They laughed.

Because everything could be bought.

Neither said the word forming beneath the sound.

Fear.

Far from the ruins, Aurelion landed hard and kept running.

Behind him, the last sanctuary beyond Darth's reach turned to ash.

Ahead of him, the world waited.

And beneath the sea, his sister moved through shadow, unaware the horizon had shifted for them both.

17

WHAT WAS NEVER MEANT TO BE SEEN

The final cipher collapsed without ceremony.

One month and twelve days after the descent, Chora stopped trying to brute-force the archive and let it open itself. Exhaustion had burned away impatience. What remained was stillness.

The file did not announce its importance.

No warning.

No encryption flourish.

Just video.

The timestamp froze her.

She knew the date.

She had felt it long before she had words for it.

The image trembled, compressed by depth, time, and deliberate degradation. The angle was wrong, skewed as if the camera had never been intended to survive.

Her parents stood within the frame.

Astraea.

Caelum.

Older.

Marked.

Cuts traced Astraea's ribs. Bruising darkened Caelum's shoulder and thigh. Nothing catastrophic. Nothing fatal. But wrong.

Chora had never seen them like this.

Never injured.

Never slowed.

They moved.

Not desperately.

Not theatrically.

Deliberately.

Their wend folded between them in a way she had never been taught. This was not doctrine. This was accumulation. Decades compressed into instinct.

One moved.

The other completed.

Force entered space and vanished.

They were devastating.

Even now.

Then she noticed the delay.

It was subtle. Almost imperceptible. Healing answered, but slower. Not refusal. Fatigue.

Overlay data surfaced.

Thresholds.

Diminishing returns.

Cumulative cost.

Wend could restore only so much.

Use it too often, and it burned away.

Use it too little, and it faded.

And when wend users had children,

Chora's breath caught.

The feed split.

Medical diagrams. Neural mappings. Growth markers she recognized instantly.

Not her parents.

Herself.

Aurelion.

The realization arrived whole.

The wend had not vanished.

It had **moved**.

Transferred.
Flowed forward.

Astraea's voice surfaced next, recorded elsewhere. Quieter. Unguarded.
"We always knew," she said. "It wouldn't last. Not all at once. Just enough."
Caelum followed.
"We sent them away so they wouldn't see it."

Chora leaned back, shaking, not from grief, but from understanding too complete to resist.

They hadn't abandoned them.
They had protected them.

The footage resumed.
Astraea faltered, just one step. Caelum crossed into it without thought.
Between breaths.
Space collapsed. Enemies ceased.
Then something moved wrong.
Too precise.
Too informed.

A lethal strike arced toward Astraea.

Caelum intercepted.
The camera lurched violently, blur, distortion, static. Chora understood then: the camera fell because the strike landed where it had been mounted.
Where her parents had been.
The last clear image was light.

Then nothing.

Silence consumed the feed.

Chora did not move.

A second file opened automatically.

Analysis.

Projection.

She felt Aurelion then, not physically, not yet, but unmistakably. Somewhere, he was seeing this too. Not through data.

Through alignment.

The final dataset was not historical.

It was predictive.

Twin resonance.

Cohesive amplification.

Strategic symmetry.

What Astraea and Caelum had been was convergence.

What their children were...

Evolution.

Outcome Probability

(Twins): Exceeds Parent Baseline by **41%**
Condition: *Balance maintained. Secrecy preserved.*

Her parents had known.
This was what they had trained them for.
What they had endured for.
What they had died for.

Not revenge.
Completion.

Chora closed her eyes.
Tears fell, not in rage, not in despair, but in reverence.
"Aurelion," she whispered.

Far away, under a different sky, he answered, not with words.
With stillness.

Together.

They would finish what their parents had delayed.
Not as weapons.
Not as ghosts.

But as the final correction Darth had never modeled.
The recording ended.
And with it, the first story closed.

The second had already begun.

Epilogue

Between Breath and Aftermath

They did not reunite first.

That was deliberate.

Correction required parallel motion, separate vectors converging only in outcome. Each twin moved alone, across different continents, through different systems that believed themselves invisible.

Chora struck through infrastructure.

Ports.

Holding companies.

Men who thought their power lived on paper.

She entered cities without arrival and exited without absence. Death followed as punctuation, brief, precise, irreversible. Bodies were left just ordered enough to imply intent, never enough to explain method.

Witnesses described pressure.

Air that behaved incorrectly.

A woman who passed beneath consequence and left nothing stable behind.

Aurelion moved elsewhere.

Archives.

Mountain facilities.

Black sites buried deep enough to forget the surface.

He did not rush.

He collapsed momentum.

Men died standing, unsure when breath had stopped cooperating. He left no spectacle. Only absence where systems once believed themselves permanent.

Together, but apart, they carved a line so disciplined it resembled inevitability rather than violence.

Then the pattern emerged.

A male signature, budgets that survived purges.

A female signature, operations that remained untouched no matter the collapse.

Not executives.

Not handlers.

Custodians.

Operatives.

Chora found the proof in a ledger that refused combustion.

Aurelion uncovered the second in a vault older than its encryption.

Darth was not an organization.

It was a **dynasty**.

Not rulers.

Not leaders.

Continuity managers.

Each generation inheriting silence, refining erasure, passing power sideways instead of forward. Even Astraea and Caelum had never seen this far into the dark.

The twins did.

Chora stood over a dying man who tried to smile through blood.

"You're late," he said.

She tilted her head.

"No. You're early."

Elsewhere, a woman watched Aurelion with recognition sharpened by fear.

"So the bloodline lived," she whispered.

He did not answer.

Wend answered for him.

By the time the Operatives understood what was happening, the map was already wrong. Assets vanished. Corridors collapsed. Communications ended mid-sentence.

Darth did not feel loss.

It felt **correction**.

The twins paused at the same moment, continents apart, breathing in sync without effort.

Not victory.

Alignment.

Their parents had been convergence.

They were succession.

And somewhere within a dynasty that had never believed in endings, a final truth settled:

This was not vengeance.

This was resolution.

Between breaths, the world re-calibrated.

It would not return to its prior shape.

BOOK II

CHAPTER I

RESIDUAL PRESSURE

The building did not lose power.

That was the mistake.

Lights stayed on. Systems reported green. Elevators continued their loops without interruption.

Inside, a man finalized a transfer he believed would outlive him.

The room was glass and steel, designed for visibility without exposure. He trusted the systems. He trusted redundancy. He trusted that nothing moved without registering.

He did not trust silence.

He felt it first, not fear, not instinct.

Pressure.

Air that failed to behave.

His breath caught, not in panic, but confusion. The room did not change.

He did.

Across the space, a reflection moved that did not belong to him.

Not a figure.

A misalignment.

He turned.

Nothing stood there.

Then his knees buckled.

Documents scattered. A glass wall fractured without impact. The man collapsed inward, lungs refusing instruction.

Between breaths, the transaction completed itself.

Elsewhere, servers logged anomalies they could not classify. No intrusion flags. No corrupted data. Only outcomes that made no sense.

Across the city, across the ocean, across a system that believed itself sovereign, someone else paused.

Felt it.

Not a summons.

A confirmation.

Book II had begun.

Not with darkness.

But with pressure that refused to dissipate...

About the Author

Gary Haywood writes fiction that examines power, discipline, inheritance, and the quiet mechanics of consequence.

His work rejects traditional hero narratives in favor of structured, system-driven storytelling, where characters are shaped by environments, institutions, and decisions made long before the story begins.

WEND: The Technique Between Breaths exists within the same thematic universe as **Death Kometh** and **Born of Two-Worlds**, continuing Haywood's exploration of duality, succession, and what survives after systems collapse.

Rather than focusing on spectacle, Haywood's narratives emphasize:

- Operational realism
- Psychological restraint
- The cost of competence
- And the danger of believing power can be owned

This novel is the first of a planned trilogy.
The remaining volumes will not soften the questions raised here.
They will finish asking them.